MICHELLE AND THE MISSING MANATEE

THE ITURIA CHRONICLES

J.B. MOONSTAR

BOOK 8

MICHELLE AND THE MISSING MANATEE

THE ITURIA CHRONICLES

J.B. MOONSTAR

DEDICATION

To my wonderful and talented artist/illustrator, Jenn Kotick; her mermaid and manatee painting was the inspiration for this book!

Dear Reader,

In my continuing chronicles of the interactions between Ituria's realm and the human world, I will relate the story of a young girl who is drawn into a world unknown as she battles a hurricane to save a young manatee. To what measures will she go and who will she meet along the way?

To rescue the manatee, she will have to trust others—something she has avoided for several years since her dad died. The walls of solitude that have been her fortress must now be broken down as she will need help from others to complete the rescue. Can she overcome her fears and learn to trust again?

Join Michelle on an exciting adventure where she and her new friends work together to save the young manatee! Only courage will save the day, and along the way she learns that there is room in her heart to care for others again, no matter who they are!

Sincerely,

Knocker,

First Guard to Ituria

Table of Contents

Chapter One

THE STORM APPROACHES

Looking out the front window, Michelle searched for the source of the siren she heard. It was different than the ones she was used to hearing in the neighborhood. *It's almost like a song.*

Emergency sirens were nothing new to her. Her mother was a paramedic at the local firehouse, so she knew that each type of rescue vehicle had different sirens depending on what action was required. Because of the approaching hurricane, all emergency personnel had been ordered to report to their posts, ready at a moment's notice to assist the residents. Yet, this siren was different and didn't sound like it was coming from the direction of town. It was coming from the river behind the house.

Michelle ran to look out the back window, searching for a rescue boat on the water, but didn't see anything. Several branches were on the ground in the back yard, broken by the high winds of the hurricane, and the damage was only expected to get worse as the day progressed.

The approaching hurricane was a category two and would most likely knock several of the trees in the back yard down once the eye reached land. Looking out toward the dock, she saw the water level on the pilings of the dock had already risen about half a foot higher than normal. The storm surge was expected to be about five feet during high tide, bringing the rising river even with, or even over, the deck.

Again the siren rang out, louder this time. *Where is this coming from, and why?* She needed to match the siren with the maker. After the accident several years ago when her dad was killed, Michelle constantly questioned anything out of the ordinary, needing to solve everything that didn't match what was normal. She knew her mind would not rest until the source of this siren was revealed. She had to find it, or she would not feel safe staying in the house alone.

Several trees near the waterline blocked a full view of the river from the house, so as the siren went off once again, she went out the back door to hear it more clearly, this time focusing on its direction. Walking around the backyard, she tried to identify the location of the sound. *It sounds like it's coming from the river, but I don't see any boats.*

Once the siren stopped, it was quiet. The last wave of wind and rain from the hurricane had passed and another would hit soon. The local bugs, birds, and other wildlife in the area were, like most human inhabitants at this point, hunkering down for the eye of the storm, now only hours away.

As she headed toward their small dock, she saw something splashing underneath. Taking a quick glance at the clouds, she figured she had half an hour until the next wave hit with its torrential rain and dangerous wind. She had time to find out what was under the dock if she hurried.

Running onto the dock, she saw a large object being pushed against the dock pilings. It was not moving on its own; the splashes were caused by the waves rocking it back and forth. Getting closer, she could see it was a manatee, but it didn't appear to be moving. She remembered recent news reports about manatees starving to death because much of the seagrass they ate had been wiped out by pollution in the river. The story caught her attention because it was so sad and very preventable. Her anger started kicking in. *Why is this allowed? Why do politicians allow pollutants to flow freely into the river, knowing the consequences?*

As she looked at the manatee closer, her anger faded as concern took over. Was there anything she could do? *Maybe it is only unconscious.* She had to know if there was any way it could be alive and then maybe she could save it. However, the only movement she could see was the waves bashing it, over and over, against the dock pilings.

Wait, there is something moving! She ran to the edge and knelt on the dock, peering underneath, desperately searching to see what could have been moving—maybe a flipper on the manatee—could it still be alive, and could she save it? Although it was only mid-afternoon, the clouds were blocking the sunlight as the next wave of the storm warned of its approach, making it harder to see under the dock.

While one side of her was screaming to get back to the safety of the house, another side had to make sure that any chance to rescue this creature was taken; she would not leave if there was a way to save it. A small beam of sunlight escaped through the clouds, lighting underneath the dock for a few seconds. A movement in the water, different from the crashing waves, changed the water patterns. *There is life there! What can I do?*

Laying down on top of the dock and putting her head underneath, she saw what had been making the movements—a baby manatee was nuzzling against the larger one. It was only about five feet long. It could not understand why its mother was not responding and kept rubbing its snout against its mom's side.

What can I do? Michelle's mind started racing. She couldn't call an animal rescue group; the whole peninsula had been ordered to stay off the roads because of the high winds—no vehicular traffic was allowed until after the storm. *Can I build something to protect it from the storm?* Around her were only some broken branches; they would not help as the water and waves rose higher and higher.

There must be something I can do! I can't just leave it!

"Don't worry, little one!" she called down to it. "I will not leave you alone. We will make it through this together!"

The small manatee looked up in fear and attempted to hide itself from Michelle, paddling this way and that, finally swimming underneath the flipper of its mother to hide, hoping this human would go away.

"No, no, don't hide. I will not hurt you!" she said in a softer voice. "I will make sure you are safe!"

Peeking out from its hiding place after hearing Michelle's gentler voice, its face could now be seen. Its eyes were wide with fear as it looked at her, using its flippers to stay close to its mom as waves crashed into them and repeatedly knocked it away. *It looks exhausted!*

Suddenly, Michelle's thoughts were jarred out of rescue mode by the noise of someone running onto the deck behind her. She quickly popped her head up and turned to see who was on their property—in the middle of a hurricane—and why.

"Oh, you found him!" came a shout as the stranger got closer. "Thank you!"

Chapter Two

A STRANGER ARRIVES

"**H**ow do you know about him and why are you out in this storm?" Michelle asked curtly. She also had a problem with strangers—no one was to be trusted. It was just her and her mom now; her world was small and compact.

"You are trespassing, so you need to leave!" she shouted at him, letting him know that he was not welcome.

"But I'm here to help!" came the reply as the teenage boy quickly knelt beside Michelle, leaned over, and peered under the dock. "We need to save this baby! Can you help me?"

Still not sure of this stranger, she asked, "How did you know he was here? You can't see him from the street. How did you know?"

The teenager looked at her in silence, assessing how to respond. Michelle just stared back at him, waiting for an answer. *Why is he running around out here in the storm? And how did he know it was here?*

The stranger had black hair, was wearing jeans and a t-shirt, and had a duffle bag hung around his shoulder down onto his left side. He looked about fourteen or fifteen years old, just a few years older than she was. His hair and clothes were soaked, but his bright green eyes were piercing, alert and ready to react to anything.

"I was told that there was a baby manatee that needed help," he stated as he watched Michelle closely and waited for her reaction. She remained silent, watching him, waiting for him to continue, to provide her an explanation on why he would be here on her dock.

Quickly looking under the dock once again, he added, "The mother has been very ill and Alleana contacted me to try rescue the baby."

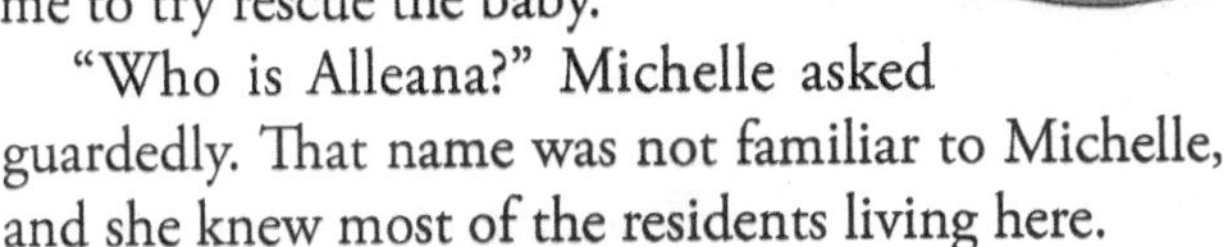

"Who is Alleana?" Michelle asked guardedly. That name was not familiar to Michelle, and she knew most of the residents living here.

"She lives in the area, and we talk on occasion. She contacted me early this morning and we have been searching since." Seeing the questions in Michelle's eyes as she stared at him, he continued, "Please allow me to introduce myself. I'm Marcus, but most people call me Knocker. Have you lived here long?"

"I've lived here for a while. I'm Michelle," she responded cautiously, still wary of this stranger. "My mom and I have lived in this house for several years now, and I haven't heard of an Alleana before, and I haven't seen you around here either."

"Nice to meet you, Michelle," said Knocker. "Please know that I mean no harm, and I have been asked to save the baby manatee. I have been told that the mother, unfortunately, was dying, and possibly already dead, but that another manatee has agreed to care for and raise the baby if we can find him and get him to safety. This little one will not survive the day if left out in the storm." Knocker's voice became tense. "The next wave of storms is about to hit, so I need to know if you will help me rescue the baby. It will involve swimming, and I'm not good at that."

Michelle paused to process all the information: *a stranger appeared and wants to rescue a manatee, he can't swim but I can, and the hurricane really complicates things.*

"Yes," she answered with resolve, knowing she couldn't leave the baby there. "I will be glad to help rescue the baby; we can't leave him where he is. Please let me know what I can do, and I will do my best!" *This tiny manatee deserves a chance at life, and I'm going to give it to him.*

"Thank you, Michelle," Knocker responded quickly. "We appreciate your help! Time is of the essence, so I must contact Alleana and let her know we have found him." He thought for a moment as he looked out over the river and continued to Michelle, "While you may be surprised at Alleana's appearance, please know that she is very kind and thoughtful and only wants to help."

Knocker stood, turned to face the river, and shouted, "Alleana, we have found him!"

Who could he be calling to? The land across from the dock is a wildlife refuge. There are no people living over there.

Peering out into the rough river surface, Michelle noticed a wake appear from something large swimming underwater, and it was coming in their direction. She had seen these wakes before, ripples on the surface of the river in a V shape, like a power boat would leave as it passed by, but there was no boat. That meant whatever was making the wake was swimming under the water's surface. She had seen this type of wake from large fish swimming just under the surface. Now she was getting worried. *What is going on?*

Okay, wake up. There is nothing swimming under the water. Your mind and the waves are playing tricks with you! Don't make up more problems!

Trying to get away from her wandering imagination, she asked, "Knocker, how did you meet Alleana?"

Knocker explained, "I met her many years ago. She takes care of the river and its inhabitants." Knocker pointed at the river. "I think I see her coming now."

"What do you mean? I don't see a boat—what are you pointing at?" Michelle's voice was full of apprehension as she looked back at the river. The water was choppy, and the wake was getting broken but kept reappearing. *It's just my imagination!*

Standing and moving next to Knocker, she looked where he was pointing—it *was* the same wake in the water that caught her attention, *and it's heading right for us!*

"Not to worry, Michelle," Knocker replied in a calm voice. "As I said before, Alleana is very nice and only needs help to get the manatee to his new family. We would not seek your help if it was not desperately needed."

As Knocker spoke, the wind gusts picked up and the rain started falling hard—the next wave of the storm had arrived!

Michelle looked at Knocker and then back to the river where the wake was still advancing, and her mind started racing. *This is getting too crazy. What is going on? How are we going to rescue the manatee in this weather? Is it already too late?*

Suddenly, a young woman's head and shoulders rose above the waves a few feet in front of the dock, bobbing up and down in the rough water. Looking at Knocker through the torrential rain, she called out, "Thank you so much Knocker. We have been looking for many hours!"

Chapter Three

Help From Under The Waves

"Who are you? Where did you come from?" Michelle shouted back to Alleana over the howling wind. She couldn't believe her eyes. *Who could be swimming in this weather?*

Not realizing there was someone next to Knocker, Alleana looked through the rain to see who was calling to her. When she saw Michelle, her eyes widened in panic. She shouted out, "Knocker, she can see me! Why did you call me when it was not safe?!" Alleana instantly disappeared under the water.

"Alleana, come back!" Knocker called into the storm. "It's safe! This human has agreed to help us!"

Surfacing about ten feet away, Alleana's eyes still filled with doubt as she looked at Michelle. "Does she know? Did you tell her?"

"No, I have not," Knocker called back. "We have not had time to discuss specifics. However, she does understand that we need to save this baby, and her strength will be needed to get this baby to safety. I feel that I can trust her, unlike many humans I have encountered before."

"Michelle," Knocker continued, getting closer so she could hear him above the downpour, "we need to know if we can trust you." The noise from the storm was so loud, he still had to shout to her. "If we are to save this baby, we will reveal secrets about ourselves that cannot be shared with others—we have no choice. Can we trust you to keep our secrets?"

Michelle looked at Knocker and then to Alleana. "If we can save this baby—if you can help—and something is revealed that others should not know, I promise I will not reveal your secrets." Nothing else mattered to her at this point other than rescuing the baby.

"Thank you, Michelle," Knocker said. "You need to know that Alleana is a mermaid. She is the leader of the mermaids of Crystal Cay. I can't help move the baby since it is in the water, and we need your help to swim with it, making sure it is breathing, and helping it to swim as Alleana takes it to a safe place where it can ride out the storm."

"What do you mean she is a mermaid—is this a joke?" Michelle called out over the rain and wind, her mistrust kicking in as she stared at Alleana. "We need to get serious here!"

"We are serious, Michelle," Knocker replied over the howling wind. "It may be hard to believe, but there is magic in this river. Alleana is one of the magical creatures that calls this river her home."

Alleana remained silent as she watched and listened to the dialogue between Knocker and Michelle. At this point, she was not sure if this rescue was going to happen, or if she should just disappear under the waves; she also had trust issues.

"Look," Michelle answered. There was no time to argue. "If she wants to believe she is a mermaid, and it helps save this little one, I'm okay with that, and I will be glad to help you. Let's do this!"

Michelle took off her sandals and put them in a little storage bin on the side of the dock as she got ready to jump into the water. Knocker reached out and touched her shoulder to stop her before she jumped.

"Wait, one more thing," Knocker said quickly. "You will need this."

Taking a small stone out of his bag, he carefully handed it to Michelle, making sure the wind and rain didn't cause it to drop into the water. "Please put this in a safe pocket so that you do not lose it. It is necessary for you to be able to talk with Alleana, and it will also let you talk to the manatee so he can understand you. Michelle, you must be within ten feet for the stone to work; you have to be close, or you won't be able to talk to each other, okay?"

Looking at the Knocker and then at the stone, she saw it was small and flat, about the size of a half-dollar coin. Although this just raised more questions, there was no time for discussion. Michelle nodded and put the stone in a pocket of her shorts that zipped, making sure the zipper was fully zipped closed before jumping into the river below.

Waves broke over her face as she surfaced, the water splashing into her mouth as she took a breath. Between the waves and rain, she would have to take special care not to swallow a lot of water. Swimming under the dock, she did her best to avoid being pushed into the pilings by the driving waves. *Knocker said I could talk to it now. Can I?*

"Little one!" she called out as she headed slowly toward the baby manatee and its mom, not wanting to frighten it. "We have come to help. Please let us help you!"

This time, the baby looked at Michelle and did not try to swim away.

Alleana joined Michelle under the dock, and they both approached the baby cautiously so it would not flee from them. "We have come to take you to a safe place," she called to it. "What is your name, little one?"

Peering out from behind his mother, he said, "I'm Ethan. I'm so afraid. My mom won't wake up." As he talked, he nudged his mother's body again with his snout.

Michelle understood him—*Maybe there is something to this magic! Does this mean Alleana really is a mermaid? Okay, something to figure out later—one thing at a time!*

Michelle watched as Alleana approached Ethan, swimming closer to him.

"Ethan, please listen to me," Alleana called to him, her voice was soft and melodic, breaking through the sound of the wind and rain, expressing her care and concern for Ethan. "We need to rescue you from the storm. Your mom was sick and called out to me to help you to safety. Come with me. It is not safe for you to stay here in this storm."

Ethan looked at his mom once more, then swam slowly over to Alleana, nodding his head. "My mom told me that … if you came … I should go with you … so I will do as she said." His voice was soft and broken, full of sadness. Alleana's arms reached for Ethan and gave him a welcoming hug, knowing how hard it was for him to leave his mother.

"Michelle," Alleana called to her, "I will need you to help me get Ethan to a small cave across the river; it is not too far. However, with the waves and rain, I need you to guide him and to make sure that he is getting to the surface to breathe. As a mermaid, I don't require surfacing to breathe, so I will rely on you."

Swimming over to Alleana and Ethan, Michelle reached out and put her hand Ethan's shoulder and looked into his eyes. "Hi, Ethan. I'm Michelle. We will make sure you are safe, okay?"

Continuing to Alleana, Michelle asked, "What if I stay on this side and hold onto him, keeping near the surface and making sure he breathes every time I breathe, and you stay on the other side and guide us through the water? Does that work?"

Alleana nodded in agreement, and they headed out from under the dock, the three of them lined up in a row, Alleana and Michelle with Ethan in the middle. Michelle glanced back at Alleana; *she does indeed have a mermaid's tail—is she really a mermaid?*

No time to worry about it now. "Okay, Alleana, I'm ready! Lead on!"

As the three started across the river, the downpour continued, and the wind gusts whipped up the waves. The rain and waves did not affect Alleana who remained under the surface. However, when Michelle and Ethan rose above the waves to breathe a few seconds later, the rainwater poured into their noses and mouths, causing them to cough and choke. *It is going to be challenging for us to breathe in this downpour. I must make sure Ethan takes a breath!*

Seeing their difficulties, Knocker called out to Michelle, "I will try and block the rain so you and Ethan can breathe a little easier!"

Looking back at Knocker, Michelle called out, "I thought you couldn't swim!"

"I can't!" he replied.

Chapter Four

ANOTHER SURPRISE

Peering at Knocker through the downpour, Michelle stopped and watched in amazement as Knocker transformed into a giant dragon, his large wings lifting him up as he flew over to hover above Michelle and Ethan in the choppy water. He positioned himself over them, holding his own against the strong winds. His body and wings blocked the rain enough to allow Ethan and Michelle to breathe between the breaking waves without inhaling the torrential rain.

"Thank you!" Michelle called out to him. "That helps a lot!" Her skepticism about the existence of mermaids and dragons would have to be put on hold until after the storm when reality would take over once more.

Reaching out for Ethan again, Michelle made sure that he was able to surface between the choppy waves and take a breath. Swimming forward and taking quick stops to breathe worked for her and Ethan, and soon Michelle and Alleana got into a swimming rhythm that Ethan could follow. *It may take a while to get across the river, but at least he is safe, and he now has a mermaid and dragon to protect him!*

Michelle surfaced with Ethan every twenty seconds or so, and as she took a breath, she looked over to make sure he took a breath too, then nodded to Alleana. After a few minutes, Ethan seemed to be struggling to get to the surface.

"Ethan, are you okay?" Michelle asked, talking loudly over the howling winds.

"I am just so tired right now. Is it much longer?" Ethan replied, his voice was stressed as he tried to keep his head above the waves.

"We are about halfway across the river," Alleana answered as she appeared next to them. "Ethan, why don't you just let us pull you along? You don't have to try and swim. Okay?"

"Okay, thanks," Ethan replied. "I just can't swim as fast as you can."

"Michelle, why don't you put your arm over Ethan's back and hold him up?" Alleana called to her. "You can make sure that Ethan is able to breathe and help him along from the surface. I will get underneath Ethan and let him ride on my back."

"Ethan," Alleana called to him. "You must let us know if this works, or if we need to make other adjustments, okay?"

"Yes, I will. Thank you!" Ethan answered, relieved that he didn't have to struggle to swim anymore.

"Ethan, are we surfacing to breath enough?" Michelle asked, concerned he wasn't getting enough air. "Should we do it more often for you?"

"No, I am able to breathe very well. Thanks!" Ethan responded.

"All right, let's try this again. I'll be underneath guiding Ethan, and Michelle, you will be next to him, helping him from the side and making sure he breathes!" Then Alleana vanished under the water and took her position under Ethan.

"Okay, Ethan. Let's do this!" Michelle called to him with encouragement, giving him a quick hug as she put her arm over his back.

As they finally made it to the other side, Michelle estimated it had taken about a half an hour to swim across the river. *Where do we go from here?*

"Michelle," Alleana surfaced and called to her. "Thank you! I will take him from here. There is a small cave just over there. Please return with Knocker before the worst of the storm gets here!"

"Michelle, follow me!" Knocker called down to her. "I will lead you back to your house!"

Looking up to the sky, Knocker was hovering over her. "Okay! Heading back now, I will follow your lead!" Michelle could just barely see her house from this side of the river, but when swimming, she could keep Knocker in her sight, and it was much easier to keep on track by watching him.

The swim took several minutes, and Michelle was glad to see her dock come into sight. The water level was about even with the deck now. The storm surge was here! With the many waves breaking against the dock, climbing back onto the deck was difficult; however, Michelle was able to do so, and Knocker hovered over her to protect her from the downpour as she started running up the deck to reach the porch.

A large crack sounded above the wind and rain, and Michelle looked around to see what was happening behind her.

"Michelle, run!" Knocker called to her as he swooped in low to shield her. Watching a large pine tree falling their way, she saw it hit Knocker, slamming him hard to the ground.

"No!" Michelle cried out as she ran back in the raging storm to the fallen tree with Knocker pinned underneath.

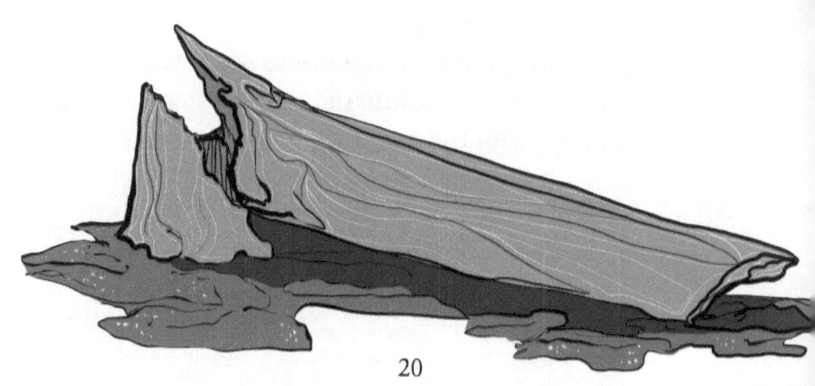

Chapter Five

KNOCKER NEEDS HELP

"**A**re you hurt?" Michelle called to him through the pouring rain. "What can I do to help get you out from under the tree?"

Michelle looked desperately at the tree laying on top of Knocker, trying to figure out what she could do. While Knocker was very large as a dragon, the branches of the tree covered most of him, including his outstretched wings. The trunk of the tree landed on Knocker's right leg, which was bent at an awkward angle.

"Knocker, can you hear me? Are you hurt?" Michelle cried out, hoping that he would answer, that he would be okay.

"Michelle, I can hear you," Knocker said slowly. "Give me a minute. That was quite a fall." Knocker's large dragon head looked around, his voice tense as he assessed the situation. "Looks like this one got me good!"

"If you hadn't tried to protect me, you would be fine—it's all my fault!" Michelle replied, distressed and panicking. *I caused this! If he hadn't tried to protect me, he wouldn't be hurt!* "That's why I never deal with people—or dragons! Someone always gets hurt! I'm so sorry! Please let me know what I can do!"

"Michelle, it was not your fault," Knocker replied, noting her panicked voice. "It was not the tree's fault either—it had no choice as it was blown over by the storm. Let's just take this one step at a time, okay? Please be calm." Knocker's voice was calm and controlled, even though he had to call out loudly to be heard over the howling wind.

"First things first, I need to get out from under this tree, don't you agree?" Knocker asked Michelle, trying to keep her from being so upset.

"Yes, of course!" Michelle answered anxiously. "But how can you do that?"

"Have you forgotten that I am a dragon?" Knocker replied.

"No, but then I've never seen a dragon before!" Michelle responded, trying to figure out what he meant. "What can you do? You are trapped by the tree!"

"Stand back. This may get a little messy!" Knocker called to her. "I'm going to move the tree, okay?"

Backing up about ten feet, Michelle called out, "Is this far enough?"

Knocker nodded his head, and then used his front legs to lift the tree off him, throwing it in the other direction so it would not hit Michelle.

"How did you do that?" Michelle asked as she ran back to his side, incredulous that he had been able to lift the fallen tree—it had to weigh several tons.

"I am a dragon, remember?" Knocker said, a little more serious this time. "Next step is to get up; however, I fear that my leg is broken. The tree came down hard on it. This may be more manageable if I transform into my human form. Please back away for a moment. This will take some concentration on my part, considering the current circumstances."

"Of course," Michelle said as she backed up and sheltered next to the side of her house. She looked around at the rain and wind and branches flying around; it was a chaotic situation indeed.

Watching closely, it took several minutes for Knocker to transform into a human. Now he looked small and vulnerable out in the yard, next to the gigantic tree that had fallen on him. Michelle ran out into the storm and kneeled next to him. "What can I do now? We need to get you some help!"

"No, human help will not do. I must return to Ituria's Island; however, I cannot do so until the moon rises over the horizon, which will not be for another hour." Knocker's voice was tense. He was trying to remain calm, figuring out what they needed to do next.

"If you could help me to your shelter, I could remain there for a short while until I can return home," Knocker said. "I will need something to lean on to help me walk."

"What will work? You need something strong!" Michelle replied. "I have some gardening tools in the garage. Let me get them. One may be strong enough!"

Jumping up, Michelle ran onto the porch and through the house to the garage. She grabbed several large gardening tools, hoping one or more would work, and ran back out to Knocker. "Will any of these work?"

Knocker was sitting up now, and he nodded his head. "I think I can use these! Just one second." Michelle watched as Knocker used his arms to move himself over to the fallen tree, then he pulled himself up into a sitting position on the trunk, wincing as he used his hands to move his leg. Taking the hoe and tilling rake from Michelle, he used them like crutches, leaning on them as he pulled himself into a standing position.

He winced again as he stood, but soon he was able to use the tools to walk slowly over to the porch, trying to keep his balance in the blowing wind. Michelle held the door as he came inside; the wind was howling and swirling around them as they entered. Once inside the porch, the direction of the wind and rain was blowing away from them, so this would be a safe place to stay, at least for now.

Michelle motioned for Knocker to sit in the large chair on the porch, then grabbed another chair to sit next to him. "How will you know when you can leave?" she asked.

"I will know when I can feel the moon's presence in the sky," Knocker replied.

Michelle's face got a confused look, and she was ready to ask another question, but she heard the phone ringing. "One moment. I'll be right back!" she called as she ran into the house.

"Hi mom," Michelle said after picking up the phone. "How are you? Yes, I'm fine... Okay, I understand. Just be safe, okay! Don't worry about me… Good night, love you!"

After the call, Michelle ran back onto the porch. "That was my mom. She will be out all night tonight. They need to stay at the station so when the storm passes, she can answer any calls that come in." Sitting down next to Knocker, she asked, "How are you now? Can I get you anything?"

"I think it would be best if I just sat here until the moon appears." Knocker was talking slowly, and his voice was very strained now. Michelle could see him clenching his jaw; he must be in a lot of pain. "Then I will be able to get home."

Knocker slowly leaned back in the chair as he looked outside at the torrential rain and winds. "The wind outside is getting stronger and louder; the center of the storm must be close. That may pose another obstacle. I may have to wait until the eye of the storm reaches us."

Michelle and Knocker watched the storm through the screen at the back of the porch. As they waited for the moon to rise above the horizon, the siren Michelle heard earlier in the day started to sound again.

Michelle turned to Knocker with a questioning look. "What is that sound? I heard it earlier today before I met you on the dock."

Knocker sat up immediately, his voice anxious and worried. "That is Alleana calling for help!"

Chapter Six

ALLEANA RETURNS

Knocker carefully stood using the garden tools and hobbled with some difficulty over to a chair at the porch screen nearest the dock. Shouting into the wind and rain, he called out, "Alleana, what is the matter?"

The siren sounded again and started getting louder.

"That is Alleana?" Michelle asked, not believing this siren was the mermaid's true voice.

"Yes," Knocker replied, his eyebrows furrowed and jaw tense. He was very worried over what he was hearing. "Alleana's natural voice would sound different to you without the translation stone, but I can understand what she is saying, and she is calling to me … asking for help!"

"What is she saying?" Michelle replied, now very concerned, knowing that something had gone wrong—they were not done yet!

"Michelle, listen to me," Knocker said, his voice was stilted and broken. "I cannot … go to the dock and talk with Alleana… you still have the translation stone … right?"

Michelle nodded, listening intently as Knocker continued, his bright green eyes staring into hers. "Can you please … go talk with her? I know it is a lot to ask … with all the rain and wind … but she desperately needs someone to help her… If you could find out what happened … maybe we can figure something out together … to help my friend, Alleana!"

"Of course, I will go!" Michelle replied. "I will see what Alleana needs and help her as best I can. You need to take care of yourself. You cannot help her in this condition."

"Thank you!" Knocker said with a brief smile, relaxing just a bit. "I am not used to being the one who needs help… This is … most difficult for me." He grimaced as he tried to move his leg to get a better view of the backyard where Michelle would be running to get to the dock.

"Remember … you have to be within ten feet of Alleana to talk with her… The translation stone only works in a ten-foot radius, okay? Please be careful!" Knocker sat back in the chair slowly, knowing he could only watch at this point, Michelle would have to take over.

"Okay!" Michelle called out as she headed out the porch door and ran down to the dock. "I'll be back soon!"

Using her hand to shield her eyes from the rain as she ran, Michelle avoided several large branches on the ground and quickly reached the dock. The dock was underwater, but she could see the boundaries by the pilings sticking out of the waves. Making her way to the edge of the dock facing the river, she called out, "Alleana, I am here!"

"Michelle!" Alleana called as she surfaced close to the dock. "Where is Knocker? I need his help!"

"Alleana, Knocker has a broken leg. He was protecting me from a falling tree. He cannot help. What can I do to help you? What is the matter?" Michelle called out as loud as she could. The wind was hurricane-force now, and the rain continued to beat down upon her.

"Fallen trees have blocked the cave. I was able to move the first away; however, others washed into the opening while I was moving the first. Now the water is rising, and I am fearful that Ethan may not have enough air to breathe!" Alleana was in panic mode. That is what Knocker heard. "Ethan is all alone and needs help now!"

"Knocker won't be able to help us. Let me see if I can find some ropes to pull the trees off," Michelle called out, trying to think of what might help Alleana. The most important thing that Alleana would need is someone to help her move the branches and Knocker wasn't available. Michelle looked up at the angry sky, not sure if she would be able to swim over there in the current conditions.

"Alleana," Michelle shouted out to her. "I can get you some ropes and tools, but I don't think I will be able to swim in these conditions. It has gotten a lot worse since we swam with Ethan, and I won't have Knocker to block the rain! What can we do?"

Swimming up to the edge of the dock, now underwater, Alleana looked at Michelle. "Michelle, friend of Knocker. Will you help me? I have the power to turn you into a mermaid for a short period of time so that you can swim under the water—it is *much* easier to swim under water during a storm. Once we have freed Ethan, you can swim back here, and then turn back into a human."

Alleana paused for Michelle to answer as the rain beat down and wind howled in the background.

Without hesitation, Michelle replied, "Of course, I will help you, Alleana, whatever needs to be done! Just tell me what I need to do!" The thought of little Ethan trapped again made Michelle ready to do anything to keep him safe.

"Thank you, Michelle!" Alleana called to her, her voice full of gratitude. "Please get your rope and tools and I will await you. Once back, I will provide you with the amulet that allows you to turn into a mermaid!"

"I'll be right back!" Michelle called as she headed back to the house. So many things were running through her mind. *Okay, I must get Knocker outside so he can go home when the moon rises, get ropes from the garage, maybe a small saw or branch cutters if there is one, then meet Alleana back on the dock. I will do this for Ethan. He needs my help now!*

Chapter Seven

THE FISH AMULET

R unning by Knocker on her way to the garage, she shouted out a quick explanation of what was going to happen.

"Knocker, Alleana will turn me into a mermaid so I can swim under water. I'm going to help Alleana remove some broken branches blocking the cave entrance to free Ethan, and I need to get you outside so that you can return home when the moon rises. Going to the garage now. Be right back!"

As she came back onto the porch with the rope and a branch cutter, she continued her conversation, "Knocker, let me move this chair to just outside the porch. You tell me the best place. Then when it is time, you can go back home to the moon, okay?" Michelle pushed a large wooden chair through the porch door and looked to Knocker for further direction.

"Yes, Michelle, you have a great grasp of the situation. Thank you!" Knocker called to her. "If you could put it a little to the west… there … that is perfect!"

Running back onto the porch, she helped Knocker get to his feet and out to the chair. "Michelle, let me thank you again." His voice was serious, but he was calmer now, realizing Michelle would be able to help Alleana in his place. "You may not understand how important this is to me, but I understand and appreciate your willingness to help me and my friends."

"I am always willing to help those in need. Helping must run in my family: my mom, my dad …" Michelle stopped for a moment, then closed her eyes and shook her head to get rid of the bad memories. Looking back at Knocker's bright green eyes, she smiled at him as she continued, "Yes, I am always glad to help!"

As Michelle ran back inside to grab the rope and cutters, she saw an umbrella next to the door and grabbed that too.

"While the wind isn't as bad on this side of the house, the rain is," Michelle yelled to Knocker as she ran outside again and set down a handful of items.

"Here is an umbrella to help you keep at least a little of the rain from hitting you!" Michelle smiled as she opened the umbrella and handed it to Knocker.

Knocker wasn't sure what to do with it at first, not knowing what it was. Michelle positioned it so that it would keep the rain off Knocker's face, and he smiled back at her. "Thank you!"

"Hold it like that so the wind doesn't blow it away, okay?" Michelle replied as she bent over to grab the rope and cutters, then she was off to the dock again.

"Please be careful, Michelle. I will be watching for your return!" Knocker called out to Michelle as she ran.

"I will, Knocker—please be safe!" Michelle replied as she raced to the dock.

Reaching the dock, Michelle called out for Alleana, who had disappeared. "I'm back now. Alleana, where are you?!"

Popping up from beneath the waves next to the dock, Alleana replied loudly so she would be heard above the wind. "Here I am! Are you ready?"

"Ready as I'll ever be—tell me what to do!" Michelle shouted back.

"Secure the items you are carrying to your belt or clip them together as you will need at least one hand to transform and navigate. Then jump in next to me!" Alleana called to her.

Michelle tied the rope to the handle of the cutters so she would only need one hand to hold both. Looking back for a moment, she saw Knocker watching her as she jumped into the water. As she surfaced, she felt a hand on her shoulder and saw Alleana next to her. In Alleana's hand was a small fabric bag with a button closure.

"You must take great care with this case and its contents. Inside is a magical amulet that will allow you to turn into a mermaid," Alleana explained.

Michelle nodded, listening attentively, she needed to make sure she got this right!

Opening the bag and pulling out a small golden fish figurine,

Alleana placed it in Michelle's hand and wrapped Michelle's fingers around it before she let go so it would not be lost in the pouring rain. "Put the bag into your safe pocket and hold the fish in your hand."

"Okay, this is what is going to happen," Alleana shouted and moved closer to make sure she could be heard over the storm. "Make sure the bag in your pocket, then while holding the fish say 'I am a mermaid' three times and *only* three times, and you will become a mermaid! Once we have rescued Ethan, you do the reverse—I am a human—three times, understand? Do you have any questions?"

Michelle looked at Alleana and then the little fish in her hand. *Is this really going to work?*

"Do you have any questions?" Alleana repeated, wanting to make sure Michelle understood.

"No questions!" Michelle answered, ready to go. Putting the bag into her pocket, she held the fish in front of her. She knew this was the only way she would be able to help little Ethan; she just hoped it worked.

Shouting as loud as she could, thinking it might help, Michelle repeated the words Alleana had instructed her to use. "I am a mermaid. I am a mermaid. I am a mermaid!" Then she waited to see what would happen next.

Chapter Eight

RESCUING ETHAN

Megan felt a tingling sensation all over her body, then she felt her legs fuse together, and a long mermaid tail appeared! Her pants transformed into a little satchel with a long handle going over her shoulder. That's where the translation stone and bag for the fish were now located. Her shirt had transformed into some type of bathing suit top, with her arms bare and free to use for swimming—or whatever mermaids use them for!

"Yes!" Alleana shouted, "it worked! Let's go now before it is too late!"

"Let's go to Ethan. I'll follow you!" Michelle shouted, still trying to get her mind around the fact that she was a mermaid now!

Michelle didn't really know how she would be able to breathe under water, but as Alleana vanished under the waves she put the fish amulet into its bag, then back into her satchel, and went under. Opening her eyes, her vision improved immensely! She could see Alleana swimming in front of her; Alleana turned and waved for her to hurry before swimming away.

Taking off after Alleana, it took her a few seconds to get her mermaid tail muscles coordinated. She was used to running or kicking with alternate legs; however, her mermaid tail required that she kick together as one extremity, not two.

Although she didn't realize it when she went under the water, she was holding her breath. When Michelle felt the need to breathe, her new form knew what to do, and automatically took in water through her nose and exhaled water out again—*wow, this is great!*

Not having to worry about the wind, waves, and rain that were causing havoc on the surface of the water, she was able to follow Alleana and they quickly got to the other side.

As they popped their heads up next to the cave, she could see Alleana was right, the cave was almost underwater, and there was a large tree and numerous branches blocking the entrance.

Ethan was crying out in distress from inside the cave, "Someone help me! I can't get out of here and the water is very high! It is hard for me to breathe!"

Calling back to him, Michelle let him know help had arrived, "Ethan, Alleana and I are here now; we are working on getting this unblocked. Hang on!"

"Okay! Thank you!" Ethan answered, glad someone had heard his calls for help. "I will do my best! Please hurry!"

Michelle wrapped the rope around the large trunk blocking the cave—they would need to pull it away! Using some large rocks near the shore for leverage, she pulled hard and moved the trunk across the water until she was able to get it far enough to create a space for Ethan get past; however, the top branches of another tree were tightly wedged into the opening as well. Michelle tied the rope so the tree trunk wouldn't slip back, then took out the branch cutters and started cutting. Alleana pulled the cut branches away from the opening as Michelle worked on making a path for Ethan.

It took about ten minutes to clear away the many branches, but finally, Ethan was able to swim to them through the opening.

"Thank you!" Ethan said as he swam out. "There was very little air left!" He swam over to Alleana and Michelle, snuggling himself in between them, wanting to hide from the storm that was still raging on the surface.

Michelle looked at Alleana, concerned about what was next. "Ethan cannot stay out here in the storm. What do we do now?"

"Yes, I agree," Alleana responded. "Will you help me to protect him until the eye of the storm gets here? If so, we can use the calm time during the eye to swim him to the manatee shelter cave. It has a high ceiling and is safe for manatees. It is a little farther away, but we should be able to make it. Then you could return to your home under the water, so even if the other side of the eye wall hits, you will be safe."

"Yes," Michelle called out to her. "In the meantime, let's see if we can find something to protect him while we wait!"

Looking around, Michelle was searching for some type of shelter for Ethan. Seeing the large tree trunk they had pulled away from the entrance, they found the small enclave it formed that blocked most of the wind and rain.

"Alleana," Michelle called out. "We can use that tree trunk we tied up over there as a shelter. Ethan can breathe under it, and it will provide some protection from the rain. Let's hope the eye arrives soon!"

Michelle swam with Ethan to the tree trunk. It formed a small ledge above the river that Ethan could stay under so the rain did not hit him. The wind was only partially blocked, however, and the waves continued to crash around him. Michelle positioned herself in front of Ethan and did her best to block the wind and waves, making sure that Ethan was able to breathe.

"We can't do this for much longer, Alleana. When will the eye get here?" Michelle called to her.

"Only a few more minutes now," she called back. "Then we must swim fast; the water will be calm but only for a short period of time. We will both hold onto him as we swim so he doesn't get tired. One important matter: even though you are a mermaid and can breathe under water now, you will still need to make sure Ethan is getting to the surface to breathe, okay?"

"Yes, of course!" Michelle responded, reaching out for Ethan to give him a hug. "Ethan, we will protect you and swim with you to a safer place. I'll make sure you can breathe. Let me know if you need more breaths, please, as I'm a mermaid now and won't need to breathe air."

"Yes, Michelle," Ethan replied softly, his voice barely noticeable above the high winds. "I will trust you to take me to a safe place! Thank you and Alleana for returning for me!"

The strongest of winds was buffeting them about when suddenly the wind and rain stopped and there was an eerie calm on the river. Michelle quickly retrieved the rope and tied it to the cutters, looping both onto her satchel, and waited for Alleana's instructions.

"Now is the time. We must go!" Alleana called out as she swam to the other side of Ethan, and the trio headed into the river, hoping to make it to a safer place before the opposite eye wall reached them.

Chapter Nine

TRIP TO THE MANATEE SAFE CAVE

Alleana took one side of Ethan and Michelle took the other, both wrapping one arm around him so they could keep pace with each other. Michelle didn't need to surface for air, but Ethan did. They swam under water for speed, but Michelle knew she needed to surface for Ethan. She counted to twenty, and at twenty, she took Ethan to the surface and called to him. "Breathe, Ethan!"

After Ethan took a breath, they went back under. Another twenty seconds, another rise to the surface, allowing Ethan to breathe. Alleana's role was to direct them to their destination, and Michelle made sure Ethan was able to breathe regularly. It took about twenty minutes to get to the larger cave that Alleana said would be safe and had a high ceiling so it would not get flooded by the tidal surge.

"Ethan, you will be safe here!" Alleana called out as they neared the cave. "There are other manatees here too, so you will not be alone."

Letting go of Ethan for a moment, Alleana swam ahead into the cave and returned quickly with several manatees close behind. "Ethan, please come here and meet your new family." She called to him softly, knowing that the events of the past few hours had been traumatic, and Ethan would need all the tender loving care that this new family could give him.

Michelle gave Ethan a big hug and said to him, "Take care of yourself, Ethan! You are a brave little manatee!" Then she let him go and he swam over to the manatees on the other side of Alleana.

"Welcome, Ethan! We are so glad you are here. We are looking forward to having you as part of our family!" said the first manatee as she went to hug him with her flipper.

A smaller manatee appeared from behind the first. "Hi, Ethan. I'm Arnie. We can be best friends and play together after the storm, okay?"

Michelle saw Ethan smile, just a little, as Arnie swam over to him.

"We need you to get back into the cave now. I can see the other side of the eye wall fast approaching!" Alleana called to the manatees. As they headed back to the cave, she turned to Michelle and continued, "Michelle, you must return to your home as fast as possible. You only have a few minutes before the other side of the eye wall reaches us. Be aware that the wind and rain will come from the opposite direction now!"

Michelle looked across the river, and she saw her house down the river on the other shore. Diving under the water, she started swimming as fast as she could. Being a mermaid was very helpful!

She could see very well under water, so she only had to surface occasionally to make sure she was heading in the right direction. *No road maps under the water!*

Reaching her dock, she saw it was still about a foot under water, so she pulled herself up and sat on the deck. She took out the small fish amulet from the bag and said quickly, "I am a human. I am a human. I am a human!"

The tingling feeling started again, and within a few seconds, she was a human! Looking around, she could see the eye wall almost upon her. She quickly put the fish amulet back into its pouch and worked her way up the submerged dock until she reached land and started running to the porch.

The eye wall hit, and like Alleana had said, the wind and rain came from the other direction—this time right onto the porch. She got to the inside of the porch and up against the wall closest to the house and then turned around, looking for Knocker.

"Knocker," she called out, "are you still here?"

A small voice responded, "Knocker said to tell you that he was able to get back home, and he will return as soon as he is able so he can help you and Alleana."

Michelle looked around. *Where did that voice come from?* There were no other people, or mermaids, around that she could see.

"I'm down here!" the voice said.

Looking down, Michelle could see a small crack in one of the boards on the porch deck, and looking closer, she saw a tiny lizard's head pop up.

"Are you talking?" Michelle said in disbelief.

"Yes, I'm Max," the lizard replied. "Knocker said you still had the translation stone and would be able to understand me, and I should give you that message when you got back home."

"Oh!" Michelle exclaimed. She had forgotten about the translation stone. "Well, thank you for letting me know. I am glad he made it back! I was worried about him and his broken leg."

"Knocker told me to tell you not to worry," Max added. "Once he is able to meet with Ituria, he will be fine!"

"Thank you, Max. Please go back into your safe place now, and I will go inside and get out of the storm!" Michelle replied as she started to open the door to the house.

"Will do!" Max called out as he jumped down into the crack in the wood where the wind could not reach him.

Michelle went into the house and put on some dry clothes. She made sure that she had a pocket that would zip on her shorts, and she put both the translation stone and the fish amulet in that pocket, closing the zipper so they would not get lost. She knew that after the storm was over, Alleana and Knocker would be back to collect them.

Chapter Ten

ANOTHER RESCUE PLANNED

Watching the storm from inside the house, Michelle could see the fierce winds and rain, and she was glad to be inside once again!

Dinner sounded good right now, so she went to the kitchen to make a sandwich. Glancing up at the clock on the wall, she noted it was almost 10:00 p.m. While she was in the fridge looking for the cheese, her mom called back.

"Hi, mom," Michelle said. "Are you okay?"

"Yep, I'm fine. Everything okay at the house?" her mom asked.

"Yep, I can see the dock is still underwater, and we lost a few trees, but otherwise we are good!" Michelle answered.

"Great," her mom replied. "I will be here for at least another eight hours or so, we are going to start handling some emergency calls now that we are on the back side of the storm. It appears to be weakening now that it is over land. I just wanted to make sure you were still safe before heading out!"

"I'm fine, mom. Please be careful, okay?" Michelle answered. She always worried when her mom was out on her emergency runs; anything could happen.

"Hey, why don't you get some sleep?" her mom suggested. "When you wake up, the storm will be over."

"Sounds good, mom. Just making a cheese sandwich and then I'll take a rest. Take care and be safe, mom!"

"I will!" her mom replied. "You, too!"

Michelle knew she would not sleep well until her mom got back home, but she would try to get a nap in while she was waiting.

Taking her plate with a sandwich and a handful of chips, she went to the back of the house and waited for Knocker and Alleana to contact her; she knew they would want to get back their magic charms. She reached into her pocket to touch the translation stone and fish, just to make sure they were still there, and that she hadn't been dreaming the whole thing!

Michelle kept her eyes focused on the storm raging in the back yard as she finished her sandwich. *How will they contact me? How long will they wait? I need to get these back to them before mom gets back!*

Remembering all that had happened—reviewing everything in her head—Michelle closed her eyes and dozed off. The sound of a siren woke her up. It was an ambulance. She knew that sound well—it was the siren her mom's ambulance used when they were heading to an accident. It sounded a few miles away, and she listened as it got farther away, heading to an emergency somewhere in the area. When it stopped, Michelle remembered that meant the ambulance had reached its destination. *Good. It means they are not driving on the road. The weather is still bad outside!*

Almost dozing again, she heard another siren, but this siren Michelle now knew was Alleana calling from the water outside. She needed help again! Michelle jumped up and ran to the back porch.

The storm was taking a short rest between waves, so Michelle ran out to the dock, glad that the deck was now about even with the water. The water was receding, returning to normal—good news! *But what does Alleana need?*

"Alleana!" Michelle called. "What is the matter?"

From behind her, Michelle heard Knocker call out, "I'm here, Alleana. What do you need?"

Michelle spun around and saw Knocker in human form running behind her on the deck—*He looks great now! What happened to his leg?*

"Knocker!" she called out with astonishment. "What happened? I thought you had a broken leg!"

"Yes," Knocker replied, talking quickly. "My leg was broken; however, Ituria has the power to heal broken bones, so once I was able to get to him, he was able to mend my leg. Didn't Max tell you?"

"Well, he said not to worry about you, but I am a worrier, so of course, I was worried! I'm glad you are okay now!" Michelle responded, relieved that Knocker was well again.

Knocker and Michelle turned to the water as Alleana surfaced in front of them.

"Knocker, I am so glad you are back!" Alleana called out to him. "A human bridge has collapsed and several manatees, including Ethan, are trapped in the cave next to the bridge! We need your strength to move the pilings and debris from the bridge. They have fallen onto the manatee's safety cave. The manatees have told me there is no way out at this time!"

"Also," she continued, "there is a human vehicle half submerged in the river. It is on top of the broken pilings. I do not know what damage the collapse may have done to the cave at this point, but the pilings falling are a bad sign. The walls inside the cave may have collapsed, too."

Michelle looked at Alleana and Knocker as they discussed the situation. *What can I do to help?* She still had some rope. Maybe Knocker could use it to pull the vehicle out of the water so he could get to the pilings?

"Hey guys," Michelle said, joining the conversation. "I have this rope. It may help you, Knocker, to get the vehicle off the pilings. Do you want to use it?"

"Thanks, Michelle," Knocker responded. "We could use some help putting it on the human's vehicle. Someone who is in the water can put it around the bottom so it will not slip out and do further damage to the pilings. Michelle, would you be able to help us? You can help me while Alleana works with the manatees trapped in the cave."

"Great idea, Knocker!" Alleana called out. "Michelle, you can use the fish amulet—you know how now. I will show you where the collapsed bridge is, and Knocker can follow us from the sky. We are in between storm waves now, but we will have to hurry. The next wave is only a few minutes away!"

Michelle took only a second to make up her mind. "Of course, I'll help if I am needed!"

Chapter Eleven

UNEXPECTED DISCOVERY

J umping into the water, Michelle pulled the fish amulet out of her pocket and said,
"I am a mermaid. I am a mermaid. I am a mermaid!"

Since she had gone through the transformation before, she knew what to expect and as soon as the transformation took place, she put the amulet back into its bag and into her satchel, and called to Alleana and Knocker, "Okay! Let's go and rescue those manatees!"

Swimming under water swiftly behind Alleana, they reached the bridge in a few minutes. Michelle was amazed how well she could see under water at night. She was able to see outlines, shapes, and movement, sort of like the night goggle viewers they show on television. *It must be a mermaid thing!*

Once they had arrived, Michelle surfaced to get a good idea of what had happened. It looked like the combination of rising water and the current washed away the dirt around the bridge foundation. The pilings were leaning, and some had fallen sideways. The weight of the vehicle, combined with the weak and leaning pilings, triggered the collapse.

The vehicle was half on the bridge and half under water. It was night and the type of vehicle wasn't readily apparent; Michelle's mermaid "night" vision revealed only that it was a large vehicle and looked like a delivery truck from a distance. None of the lights on the vehicle were working; they must have shorted out in the water. Michelle swam closer to see if the people in the truck were still there or if they had been able to get back to land.

When she got to the side window on the passenger side of the cab she looked inside—her mom was inside and unconscious!

"Knocker, it's my mom!" Michelle called out in a panic. "Help me get her out!" She tried opening the door, but it would not open. She kept yanking on it without any luck! "I have to get her out!"

"Michelle, is there anyone on the driver's side?" Knocker asked, yelling over the storm.

"No, just her! We have to get her out!" Michelle was yanking on the door in the water. It wasn't working!

"Okay, Michelle, you need to remain calm!" Knocker replied. "One step at a time. First, we need to get this vehicle out of the water. Can you tie the rope around the vehicle? You will need to swim around it, making sure it gets tied to the wheels, so it won't slip!"

Focus, focus! Get the ambulance out of the water first!

"Yes, Knocker!" Michelle called back, diving under the water to see where the rope needed to be attached. Looping it around both front tires, she doubled back behind and looped once more, then swam to the surface to hand the rope to Knocker.

Once he had both sides of the rope firmly in his claws, Knocker started flapping his wings, slowly lifting the ambulance, and pulling it back onto land. The vehicle leaned a little as he pulled, so he stopped to allow it to rock back into an upright position.

Michelle watched as Knocker carefully placed it fully on land. Swimming over to the water's edge, she suddenly realized she couldn't get out of the water as a mermaid! Placing her hand into her pocket, she felt for the little fish. Once she located it, she held it in her fingers while still in her pocket and shouted, "I am a human. I am a human. I am a human!" She hoped it would work if she was touching it as she was afraid to take the bag and fish out of her pocket amid the crashing waves.

As she felt the tingling sensation, she breathed a sigh of relief—it worked! Jumping up as soon as the transformation was complete, she ran over to the ambulance.

Now that the water was not holding the door closed, maybe she could open it!

"Mom!" Michelle yelled as she reached the door and pulled it open. "Mom, are you okay?" But her mom did not move. She reached in and took her mom's shoulders and cried out, "Mom, can you hear me?" Still no response.

Running into the middle of the road, Michelle shouted to Knocker, "Knocker, she won't wake up. What can I do?"

"Michelle, is she breathing?" Knocker shouted back.

"Yes, she is!" Michelle replied in panic mode once again. "What do I do?"

"Michelle, is there anyone else in the driving side of the truck?" Knocker called back, trying to get Michelle to focus on the situation at hand.

"No, there is on one else!" she replied. "Where could they have gone?" Another unanswered question for Michelle to worry about!

"Michelle, listen closely to me," Knocker called back, trying to get her out of panic mode. "If there is no one else in this vehicle, then they have gone for help for your mom and will be back soon. We must complete our mission to rescue the manatees before they get back!"

"But what about my mom?" Michelle responded in desperation.

Chapter Twelve

COMPLETING THE MISSION

"**M**ichelle, you must remain calm. It is the only way to help your mom and the manatees!" Knocker answered, trying to bring her back to a rational frame of mind. "If you help me finish the mission, I will do everything in my power to help your mom. It should only take a few minutes to move the pilings. Leave your mom in the shelter of the vehicle for now. That is where she is safest. Can you help us complete our mission?"

Looking at her mom, and then looking into the water where Alleana was waiting, Michelle realized she was the only hope the manatees had of getting out of the cave. "Yes, Knocker, I will help you and Alleana!" she called out to him with a new determination.

Opening the door to the ambulance, she leaned in and kissed her mom. "Mom, I love you. I'll be back soon!"

She closed the door gently to keep the wind and rain off her mom and went to untie the rope from the vehicle. Then she ran to the edge of the water, wading in until she was waist deep. Putting her hand into her pocket, she touched the fish and called out, "I am a mermaid. I am a mermaid. I am a mermaid!"

As soon as the transformation was complete, she swam around the broken pilings, wrapping the rope around one of the fallen ones so that Knocker could lift it out. "Okay, Knocker, the first is ready!" she called out to him as she held the rope ends into the air for him to grab.

Flying down to Michelle, Knocker gently took the rope and lifted the first piling and moved it to the ground far away from the cave, so the weight would not break the roof of the cave where the manatees were hiding. He pulled the rope off once the piling was moved, so he could get the rope and take it back to Michelle.

"Here you are, Michelle!" Knocker called out to her as he dropped the rope next to her. "Only a few more!"

"Alleana," Michelle called out to her, "are the manatees okay?"

"Yes, they are! I am able to talk with them," she replied. "Once we can get the pilings away from the entrance and clear a path, they will leave the area."

Swimming over to the second fallen piling, Michelle tied the rope around it, then signaled for

Knocker to grab the rope. "Got it!" he called out. "One more out of the way!" He flew it over to the first piling, dropping it and pulling the rope out to return to Michelle.

Two more pilings were removed, and there was enough of a path to start getting the manatees out.

"Michelle, you help Alleana get the manatees out, and I'll check on your mother!" Knocker called out as he turned and flew to the ambulance.

Alleana swam into the cave, and called to Michelle, "We will need to guide each one out. There is only a small opening. It will be close!"

"Okay, you start with the first, and I will go in for the next one," Michelle agreed.

Michelle watched at the entrance as Alleana lead Arnie from the cave and called out once they were out, "Okay, Alleana, I will get the next one!"

The wind and rain had subsided for a few minutes, so it was easier for Arnie to breathe while in the river. Michelle swam through the underwater tunnel to the cave and saw that the roof of the cave was indeed cracked. Surfacing to talk with the manatees, she said, "Listen, everyone needs to get as close to the front as you can. We will lead you out as quickly as possible." Pointing to the cracked roof, she continued, "Watch that crack, and if it gets any bigger, please call out to us!"

"Ethan, why don't you come with me now, okay?" Michelle said, trying to sound calm, so he would not worry about going back out into the storm. "Arnie is out there already."

"Okay, Michelle," he responded nervously, swimming closer to her.

"Ethan, I will hold you and help you swim fast okay, so you don't have to worry about taking a breath!" Michelle replied.

Wrapping her arm around him, Michelle took off through the tunnel, making sure they went fast enough to get out within twenty seconds. "There, you can breathe now!" She said to him as she smiled and gave him a hug. "Let's go over with Arnie, okay?"

"Alleana," Michelle called to her, "the roof is cracking inside the cave. You may need to get the remaining manatees out in one trip. They should be able to follow each other with you in the lead, and swim fast enough to get through the cleared path."

"If the roof is cracking, I agree!" Alleana called back. "The remaining manatees are adults and should be able to make it through following each other."

"I'll stay with Ethan and Arnie until you are all out!" Michelle called over to her. "But you need to hurry, it sounds like another wave of the storm is very close!"

Alleana led the remaining manatees through the tunnel and out to the open waters, and they gathered around the two young manatees.

"Thank you both for rescuing us," one of the adult manatees called to them. "We will head upriver where the storm should be less intense. Please keep yourselves safe!"

"Mission accomplished. Michelle, thank you!" Alleana called out to her, giving her a warm hug. "Your help was greatly appreciated!"

"I am always glad to help when I'm needed," Michelle replied, returning the hug. "Now, I need to get back to my mom!"

Swimming quickly to the shore, Michelle transformed back into a human and ran onto the road where the ambulance was placed by Knocker. She opened the passenger door, but her mom was gone!

"Knocker!" Michelle called out frantically. "Where is she?"

KNOCKER RETURNS

"Knocker had to leave," Michelle heard a deep voice call out to her, "and he asked me to wait here until you arrive and give you a message. Are you Michelle?"

Michelle looked around, confused as to what could be talking to her. Then she remembered talking to Max at the house, so she looked down. Through the rain and wind, she saw something large moving toward her on the ground a few feet away. It was dark outside, so she wasn't sure what the shadow was.

"I'm Michelle, yes!" she called out to the shadowy figure through the rain. "Please let me know Knocker's message! Is it about my mom?"

"Hi, Michelle. I'm Franco," the voice said as it got closer. "Knocker said that he was going to take your mom to visit Ituria and the healers on Ituria's Island. He will be back soon. He says to please wait for him here."

"Thank you, Franco. I will wait here for him." Michelle replied quickly. "Please go back and be safe from the storm."

"Yes, Michelle, I will go back into the river now. Be safe!" the shadow said as it disappeared into the darkness.

Michelle ran over to the side of the ambulance facing away from the blowing wind and rain, sitting down to wait. With so many thoughts running through her head, she didn't know where to start. *My mom—is she okay? How will I get home? What is going to happen next? What is taking Knocker so long? Where is he?*

Waiting for what seemed like hours, but was only about fifteen minutes, she saw a blue flash of light and saw Knocker standing in front of the ambulance as a human, holding her mother in his arms.

Jumping up and running over to them, she cried out, "Knocker, is she okay?"

"Michelle," Knocker replied, "I have conferred with Ituria, and your compassion and bravery were exemplary today. You are worthy of our trust. Ituria agreed with me and has healed your mom's injuries from the accident."

Looking at her mom, motionless in Knocker's arms, she shouted anxiously over the wind and rain, "But she is still unconscious! Is she okay?"

"Yes, Michelle, she will be fine," Knocker replied in a calm voice. "Most humans fall asleep when they travel through the vortex. She will be awake in a few minutes. She was awake for a few moments while I was talking to Ituria; I'm sure she will remember it as a crazy dream." Smiling at Michelle, he walked over and put her mom back into the passenger side of the ambulance. "She will wake up in a few minutes, and neither of us should be here, okay?"

"Can't I even make sure she will wake up? Can't I talk to her?" Michelle asked, still not convinced her mom was safe.

"No, it is better…" Knocker started, but he stopped to listen through the rain to an ambulance siren in the distance, coming their way.

"Michelle, the driver must have gone for help, and now they are on their way here to rescue your mom," Knocker said, the urgency in his voice had returned. "You must turn into a mermaid and leave for your home now. I will stay in the shadows and make sure your mom is well taken care of—please trust me!"

Michelle knew that Knocker was right, that she had to get home, but trust wasn't something she had much of these days. Listening to the siren get closer, she realized that she would need to leave before they got here. There would be no way to explain her presence at the accident scene. *But what about my mom? I need to know she is okay!*

"Okay, I will leave, but please come to my house and let me know what happens!" Michelle pleaded with him.

"Michelle, please trust me," Knocker replied. "I will make sure nothing happens to your mom. She will be fine!"

Tears started falling from Michelle's eyes as she tried to explain. "I have a hard time trusting anyone. I'm sorry. Since my dad died, I just don't trust anyone anymore."

"Look at me, Michelle," Knocker said. "You have a friend in me, and you can always trust me, okay?"

"Okay, Knocker, I will trust you," Michelle answered slowly, looking back at him. "It's nice to have a friend."

The siren was getting closer, and they both turned to see flashing lights heading their way. They were very close now.

"I guess I should be on my way," Michelle said, anxiously looking to the ambulance where her mom lay motionless, then heading for the water. "Please remember to come back to the house and let me know what happened!"

"I'll see you soon, Michelle!" Knocker called to her as she walked toward the water. As Michelle transformed into a mermaid and dove under the waves, Knocker went behind several large trees, so he could watch what transpired without being seen. Michelle stopped and surfaced about fifty feet off-shore, watching from the darkness. She needed to know what was happening, that her mom would be rescued! *I have to make sure they find her!*

When the ambulance pulled up, several men jumped out and one ran over to the crashed ambulance and looked in the passenger window. "There she is!" shouted the first. "Let's get her out and onto a stretcher quick!"

The other men pulled a stretcher out of their ambulance and rolled it over to the first ambulance.

Michelle's mom opened her eyes and looked around, trying to figure out what was going on. "Oh, hi Mike. Thanks for coming back for me!" she said in a confused voice, still trying to wake up.

"Hey, lady, what are you doing sleeping on the job?!" Mike replied with a chuckle, glad she was awake and recognized him.

"Okay, boys," Mike called out. "Let's get her to the hospital. Great to see you're awake now!"

"Hey, Mike," one of the men replied. "I thought you said the ambulance was half in the water. I wonder how it got moved!"

"We can worry about all that in the daytime. Let's get her checked out!" Mike replied.

As the ambulance with Michelle's mom left the scene, Michelle disappeared underwater and swam as fast as she could towards her home.

Chapter Fourteen

HOME AT LAST

Michelle swam as fast as she could, surfacing periodically to make sure she was going in the right direction. Her mermaid eyes allowed her to see shapes and movement in the dark, so she didn't run into anything under water.

When she surfaced near her dock, the rain and wind had subsided, so she was able to pull herself onto it and transform back into a human. This time she whispered the words just in case any neighbors were out viewing damage during the calm before the next wave of rain hit. "I am human. I am human. I am human!"

Once she transformed back into her human self, her eyesight changed, and she realized that the power had gone off in her neighborhood. None of the houses had any lights, and the streetlights were also out.

Michelle knew it was expected in hurricanes to lose power, so that didn't worry her unduly; it would be fixed once the utility crews came out in the next day or so. The problem was finding her way to her house in the middle of the night with a storm overhead in total darkness. At least the dock had small solar-powered guidelights on each of the wooden pilings, and they would lead her off the water and into her backyard. But what then?

The water had receded below the deck, so the top of the deck was visible under the small lights, and she was able to make it off the river and to the edge of the dock where it met the backyard. There she stopped as questions raced through her head. *How am I going to get back to the house? How will I find my way through all the fallen trees and debris in the yard? How will I get inside to get a phone call from my mom telling me she's okay? I need to be there when that call comes in or she will worry about me!*

Michelle started slipping into panic mode, then remembered Knocker and Alleana and how they remained calm and kept going, no matter what obstacles were thrown at them. She must complete her mission, and her mission was to get inside so she could be there when the phone rang, her mom calling to let her know that she was okay. *What is the immediate problem—I need some type of light—okay, what is available?*

Looking in the direction of the house, now hidden in darkness, she knew that she wouldn't be able to make it without a light. She remembered all the broken branches and the fallen tree from when she left. She would not be able to get through the yard without seeing what was there, and who knew what else may have flown into the yard on the violent winds. She turned and looked back at the dock with its tiny dots of light outlining the decking. *Can I use those?*

Michelle remembered a few weeks ago she helped her mom replace one of the lights. The individual light itself slipped into a holder, and then a clip snapped on top to keep it in place. Could she remove the clip and use the lights to find her way home?

She got to the first light and kneeled in front of it. Snapping the clip up, she pulled out the small light and held it in her hand. It did not give off much light, but maybe if she got several together, it would be enough. Standing up to view the available lights, she tried to figure out how many she would need. She still needed to be able to see the outline of the dock, in case Alleana or Knocker are looking for her! *I will take several from the right side of the dock, so that I know that if I stay to the left side, I won't fall into the river—that will work!*

Putting the first light into her pocket, she went to the next, unclipping and pulling it out; she repeated this until she had six small lights. She laid them next to each other on the deck and saw that together that would be enough light to get to the porch. But how would she hold them to reach the porch? She could only hold one in each hand, especially if another wave hit with its wind and rain.

The lights themselves were about three-square inches with a small loop on one side used to slide them in and out of their holders. The loops were metal and less than half an inch wide, so she couldn't slip her fingers into the loop to hold several in one hand. There must be a way to get them all pointed in one direction. She looked around her on the dock. What was available? Reaching up to wipe the dripping water out of her eyes from her soaked hair, she got an idea!

This is a crazy idea, but no one will see me, and I can take them out once I get to the porch! Reaching back, she pulled off the elastic tie holding her waist-long hair and stuck it in her pocket. Then she pulled all her hair to the front and divided it into six sections. For each section, she slipped the loop from the light onto it, and then made a loose knot on the other end. *This is crazy. I sure hope no one sees me!*

The wind and rain from the next wave were not far away now; she could hear the rain pounding down the street and the wind blowing through the trees. Positioning the lights so they all faced forward, she set out running toward the porch.

It's working! Even though the lights were small, there was enough light to show her what was in front of her, where the broken branches and trees were, and she also saw several pieces of wood and roof tiles in her backyard that she avoided.

Once the wind and rain hit again, she knew she had to hurry. Grabbing her hair at the knots so they would not untie, she started running toward the porch. Making her way onto the porch, she made up a new mission: *okay, first find the flashlight, and second, take these out of your hair before anyone sees you!*

Reaching for the flashlight on the porch, she heard the sound she was both desperately waiting for and at the same time dreading—the phone was ringing! As long as she didn't know anything for certain, her mind could convince her that her mom was going to be okay. Now she would know, one way or the other! Michelle took a deep breath, turned on the flashlight and ran inside, hoping that it was good news!

Chapter Fifteen

MOM IS SAFE

Dripping wet from the rain, Michelle ran as fast as she could to the kitchen and picked up the phone. "Hello?" *Remember, I don't know about the accident! Let them tell me what happened!*

"Hello, this is Mr. Mike. Is this Michelle?" asked a voice over the phone.

"Yes, this is Michelle. Hi, Mr. Mike, is something wrong? Is my mom okay?" Michelle held her breath, waiting for him to answer.

"Well, we had a little accident a bit ago, but she seems to be doing fine now. The doctor says we should keep her overnight at the hospital, so I wanted to let you know," Mike replied.

"Can I talk to her?" Michelle asked, still anxious. She needed to be sure.

"Sure, she's right here. Let me get her on the phone," Mike said.

Michelle listened to muffled noises, waiting for her mom. She would not be sure until she heard her mom's voice!

"Hi Michelle," her mom said, sounding a little tired. "How are you doing?"

"Hi Mom," Michelle replied, trying to remain calm. "How are *you* doing—Mike said you were in an accident. Are you hurt?"

"No, I'm fine!" she replied. "Mike said that I was unconscious when he left me, so the doctors want to run some tests, just to make sure everything is okay. I feel great, really, so don't you worry!"

"Mom, are you sure? What happened?" Michelle asked. "You know I worry!" She tried to sound light-hearted, but her voice contained her anxiety; she was still worried since her mom was at the hospital.

"And I worry about you too, dear!" her mom replied. "I've heard reports of all the power being out in our area—how is our house?"

"Well, the power is out in the house—all houses on our street—and the streetlights are out too," Michelle answered. "I do have flashlights and the battery-powered lamp to put in the kitchen, so I should be fine. Does the hospital have power?"

"The hospital is running on generators," she responded. "We should be good until the power comes back on. I'm planning on coming home some-time tomorrow, and I'll call you in the morning once they've done all their tests and can give me a time when they will be releasing me, okay? Mike said he would bring me home once I got the 'all clear' from the doctors."

"Okay, mom. It's great to hear your voice! When Mike said you were in an accident, I just panicked for a minute. You know me!" The relief in Michelle's voice was finally coming through. Her mom was okay! "You just rest and take care of yourself. I'll be here in the morning waiting for your call. I'm so glad you're okay! Love you!"

"Love you, too," her mom replied. "Talk to you in the morning. Now get some sleep!"

"Okay, mom. You, too!" Michelle said. "Good night!"

Michelle knew her mom's recovery was due to Knocker; he had taken her to Ituria to be healed. She needed to thank him and hoped he would be here soon, wondering how he was doing with the storm and how he would find his way to find her house with the power out.

She set up the battery lamp in the back room next to the porch. It was very bright, lighting up the entire back room and porch area. As she walked onto the porch with the flashlight, she saw that the rain had stopped again, so she shined the flashlight outside, trying to see if Knocker was back yet.

"Knocker!" she called out into the darkness. "Are you out there?"

"Yes, Michelle," she heard him reply from just outside the porch. "I returned a few minutes ago. Did you hear from your mom yet? I saw you talking on the phone with someone, so I waited outside."

"Yes, I did. She said she is fine," Michelle said as she stepped outside the porch door. "They want to keep her overnight for tests at the hospital, but she sounded fine! I want to thank you so much for your help today in making sure she was okay. You saved her!" Michelle's voice was full of relief and gratitude.

"I did what was needed to help my friend," Knocker replied sincerely. "You helped us with several serious situations today, and I am glad to return the favor. That is what friends do! I checked in with Alleana on my way back, and she says the manatee family is safe now. The water levels are returning to normal, and hopefully by morning the river will be quiet again."

"All I can say is that I am glad to have you as my friend!" Michelle responded with enthusiasm, then continued a with a softer voice, "And thank you again for saving my mom. Since my dad died, I really don't have any friends. It's just me and my mom now."

"I am glad to call you my friend, Michelle. Friends on Earth are hard to find for creatures such as myself," Knocker replied. "By the way, I really like the lighted necklace you have. It is very beautiful!" Knocker added, "and very appropriate for the weather tonight!"

Chapter Sixteen

SAYING GOODBYE

Looking down at the lights still hanging from her hair, Michelle laughed and started untying them and putting them into her pockets, replying. "Oh, please don't look at these. They're silly. This was just my way of creating enough light to see through the yard and get to the porch. Once I transformed back into a human down by the river, my eyesight changed so that I couldn't see anything past the dock. Together, these little lights gave me enough light to get home!"

"That was clever of you to use the lights from the dock. And it does look like a very pretty lighted necklace," Knocker said with a smile, then added in a serious voice, "Michelle, thank you for helping Alleana when I could not. I am not usually the one who needs help, but when I needed you, you were there for me and my friends. Please know that if you ever need anything, we will be glad to help you. Just let us know!"

Heading into the back yard, he continued, "If all is well with you now, I will head back to Ituria's Island. But know this, my friend, if the moon is out and you need me, call to Guardian, and he will let me know."

"What do you mean? If I call out to the moon, 'Guardian, I need Knocker,' he will hear me?" Michelle asked as she followed him into the yard, once again lost in confusion about how all of this worked.

"Yes," Knocker replied, "that is exactly what I mean. Now, if you could please return the translation stone and go back inside the house so I know you are safe, I will return to the moon. Please know that you will always have my deepest gratitude and my trust."

Reaching into her pocket and pulling out the stone, she placed it in his hand and held his hand in hers for just a moment as she responded. "Please know that you also have my deepest gratitude and trust, and I will be glad to help you and Alleana if ever I can do so." Then she stepped back, knowing he would need to transform into a dragon to go back to the moon.

"One more question," she called out to him. "How will I get Alleana's amulet back to her? Did she say anything to you about that?"

"She will be in touch with you!" Knocker called back. "You know her voice now, so if you hear that, go to the dock and call to her!"

Michelle nodded and went back inside the house, leaving Knocker in the darkness of the backyard where she knew he would be turning back into a dragon for his return trip. She watched through the back window as a blue beam of light formed heading to the sky, lighting Knocker in his dragon form as he flapped his wings in a forward motion. Then she heard a loud growl, and he disappeared along with the blue light.

Michelle sat on a couch on the porch, waiting to hear Alleana call to her. It had to be at least two in the morning, but she was not sure if she could get to sleep as she went over the many events of the past twelve hours. The siren that she heard yesterday afternoon and the many things that had happened since kept replaying in her mind.

Hearing the mermaid's siren once again, Michelle woke with a start and realized she must have dozed off. The sun was just breaking over the eastern horizon, and the storm had passed through.

Realizing Alleana was looking for her, she jumped up immediately, heading to the dock. First, though, she checked her pocket to make sure the small fish amulet was still there—that is what Alleana would be looking for—then she ran down to the river. Reaching the edge of the dock, she called out, "Alleana, I'm here!"

Alleana's head popped up in the water, and her melodic mermaid voice replied; however, because Michelle didn't have the translation stone anymore, she could not understand her.

Alleana spoke again, and this time Michelle held out her hands and shrugged, then pointed to her ears, hoping Alleana would realize that she couldn't understand mermaid speak.

Nodding her head in understanding, Alleana motioned for Michelle to join her in the water. Michelle looked around, making sure no one else was watching, then jumped into the water. As she surfaced, Alleana swam to her and held her fingers together to form the shape of a fish. Michelle understood she was looking for the fish amulet and pulled the bag containing the amulet out of her pocket and offered it to Alleana.

However, Alleana shook her head, and pointed to Michelle. *Does she want me to become a mermaid again?* Michelle pointed to the fish and to herself with a questioning look on her face. Alleana nodded. She wanted Michelle to use the fish amulet to become a mermaid again.

Michelle was glad to have one more chance to be a mermaid. Holding the fish in her hand, she said, "I am a mermaid. I am a mermaid. I am a mermaid!"

Waiting the few seconds until the transformation took place, she looked around to find Alleana, and she realized with Alleana there were several other girls swimming in the water with her. *Are they all mermaids?*

"Hi, Alleana. Thank you for allowing me to be a mermaid one more time. What an exciting experience!" Michelle called to her. "I know you are back to get your amulet, so as soon as I turn back into a human, I will return it. Please let me first thank you for your assistance in saving young Ethan. He would not have survived without your help!"

"Michelle, I wanted to thank you for your help, your bravery, and your trust in Knocker and myself.

Without you, our mission would not have been successful. I have talked with my sisters, and they have joined me in extending an invitation for you to join our pod here at Crystal Cay." Alleana turned and pointed to the others in the water around her. "I have told them of your bravery and dedication, and your empathy for little Ethan, and they have indicated that you are worthy of joining our pod."

Chapter Seventeen

A NEW DAY

Michelle looked around her. All the mermaids were smiling at her, waiting for her answer. "Alleana, I am deeply honored, but I must stay with my mom. However, I will be glad to help you and your pod whenever there is a need. All you need do is call to me."

"I know that your bond with your mother is strong, so I do understand," Alleana replied as she swam over to Michelle. "We thought that might be your choice, so we have decided that as long as you do not share your knowledge of our pod with anyone—not even your mother—you can keep the fish amulet. This way, you can join us as a mermaid whenever you are able. You will always be welcome, and you will have the amulet if there is a need for us to call you for help."

"That sounds wonderful!" Michelle called out to Alleana and all the others surrounding her. "Thank you for your friendship and trust! I would love to be a mermaid and visit you when I can, and I will be glad to help whenever you need me. I am honored to be considered your friend."

"We will need to leave now, so that we are not visible to the other humans," Alleana replied, swimming over and giving her a hug. "Welcome to my pod, my friend Michelle, and the mermaids of Crystal Cay welcome you as their friend! Take care and stay safe!"

Then, as if they were never there, all the mermaids disappeared under the water and vanished from sight. Michelle touched her fish amulet and whispered, "I am a human. I am a human. I am a human!" Once she was human again, she got out of the water and headed back to the house. *I need to find a way to always keep this amulet with me! However, now I need to get back inside and wait for my mom to come home.*

Walking back onto the porch, Michelle looked around and realized she had a few things to do before her mom got back. She quickly changed into some dry clothes, then started cleaning up any water dripped onto the floor. The tools from the garage also needed to be returned, and she would also have to put the lights back in their little containers on the dock.

Keeping busy for a couple of hours washing clothes and getting the house ready, she finally received the call that her mom was on her way home. Michelle went out to the front yard to wait for her, wanting to see her once again and give her a big hug.

Mr. Mike's car approached and parked in the front driveway. As soon as it stopped, Michelle ran over to the passenger side and opened the door, giving her mom a big kiss and hug. "Mom, I'm so glad you're okay and back home!"

"I'm glad to see you too, Michelle. We made it through another one, didn't we?!" she said as Michelle helped her out of the car.

Michelle waved to Mr. Mike. "Thanks for taking care of her and bringing her home!" she called out to him. He waved to them and headed back out of the driveway.

"Well, mom, I think you should take it easy today and go take a nap. I will make us some lunch when you wake up." Michelle kept her arm around her mom's waist as she walked her to the house.

"Okay, that sounds like a plan!" her mom replied. "Cheese sandwiches and chips sounds good to me! You wouldn't believe the crazy dreams I had when I was waiting for Mike to come back. I must have hit my head hard because I dreamed that I saw a dragon and a unicorn, and they were talking to each other! Imagine that!"

Mom chuckled and continued as she smiled at Michelle, "You know, Michelle, I also dreamed you visited me while I was in the ambulance, and you give me a kiss and told me you loved me! That's when I knew everything would be okay. I know you always worry about me when I'm out, and now I know that your love will find me—no matter where I am!"

"Mom, I'll always worry about you—just like you worry about me. It's because I love you," Michelle replied as she gave her mom a warm hug. "Now how about that nap? I'm sure they didn't let you sleep much in the hospital with all the tests and stuff."

"Yes, Michelle, you are right about that. I didn't get much sleep at the hospital, and I'm more than ready for a nice nap in my own bed," her mom responded as they walked into the house.

Walking together to her mom's bedroom, Michelle said, "Okay, you take a nice nap, and we'll eat when you get up. I may take a short nap on the couch out here too, so wake me if you need anything. It was little hectic here with the storm going through last night and the lights going out. I don't think I slept too much either."

As Michelle walked out to the back room and laid down on the couch, she thought about everything that happened over the last day: helping Alleana rescue Ethan, her mom's accident, the trapped manatee family, Knocker taking her mom to Ituria, Ethan and his new family, and lastly remembered with a smile that she had made two new friends.

She looked forward to swimming with Alleana and her mermaid friends again, and maybe even finding Ethan to see how he was doing. She also hoped that if Knocker needed help while he was on Earth, he would let her know. Remembering the many crazy ups and downs of the day, she fell asleep. It had been a long night, and she dreamed of all the great adventures to come!

THE END
until the next adventure of
Michelle and the Mermaids of Crystal Cay!

Note From The Author

While this may be a fantasy fiction novel, the record deaths of manatees are real. Over ten percent of the manatee population died in 2021, so far over 1,000 manatees, and that is not the complete count, as when this count was taken, the year wasn't over yet. That beats the record of 830 casualties in 2013. One of the reasons for the deaths is starvation as cold weather, stress, and pollution have killed tens of thousands of acres of the seagrass eaten by manatees as one of their food staples.

When manatees congregate at warm-water sources for the winter, they depend on seagrass to survive. Runoff from agriculture and industry on land causes excess nitrogen and phosphorus levels in the water, allowing for algal blooms on both the east and west coasts of Florida. These algal blooms contribute to the killing of seagrass essential for manatee survival, causing many manatees to weaken and die of starvation.

It is important to address excessive runoff from agricultural, industrial, and residential sources to clean up the water and allow the seagrass to thrive again, to help the manatees survive. This record death toll of a protected species is another example of how widespread pollution of nature's resources is threatening the native wildlife. We are only fooling ourselves if we think this pollution does not affect our own health and well-being.

More Than 1,000 Manatees Have Died in 2021 | Defenders of Wildlife November 17, 2021

Link–https://defenders.org/newsroom/more-1000-manatees-have-died-2021

Book Club Questions

1. Why is Michelle worried about the weather as she goes down to the dock?
2. How does Knocker know about the missing manatee?
3. What is the name of Alleana's mermaid pod? Where do they live?
4. What does "storm surge" mean when related to a hurricane and why would it affect the river and water level at Michelle's dock?
5. What is the "eye" of the hurricane, and why is the weather calm in the "eye"?
6. Are manatees considered fish or mammals? How can you tell?
7. What did Michelle use to light her way from the dock to her house after the power went out?
8. How did Knocker tell Michelle she could contact him if she needed him in the future?
9. Something to think about—why is it important to stop polluting the waterways? What purpose do waterways play in the natural ecosystem? How do manatees affect their ecosystem, and what other river inhabitants would be affected detrimentally should they not survive?

About the Author

J.B. moved to Florida in her early teens and has lived there ever since, enjoying the mild weather and abundance of wildlife. She even spent several seasons raising orphan squirrels. She graduated from the University of Central Florida and has spent her working career in the legal profession. Her novels are inspired by her family and nature as well as her need to escape from the real world once in a while.

www.facebook.com/J.B.Moonstar
Instagram@J.B.Moonstar
Twitter@jb_moonstar
Jbmoonstar.author@gmail.com
Website – jbmoonstar.com

Discover more by JB Moonstar

Chronicles of Ituria

Russ and The Hidden Voice

Taylor and the Red Wolf Rescue

Jenna and the Legend of the White Wolf

Jenna and the Eyes of Fire

Jan and the Secret Cave

Jan and the Search for Lilya

Taylor and the Final Nine

Michelle and the Missing Manatee

Jenna and the Broken Promise

Sara and the Secret Mission

& More Adventures to Come!

The Mermaids of Crystal Cay

Kimmi and the Sea Dragon

Roselia and the Ancient Warriors

& More Adventures to Come!

Coloring Book from

Artist Jenn Kotick

Mermaids

Discover more at
4HorsemenPublications.com

10% off using HORSEMEN10

www.ingramcontent.com/pod-product-compliance
Lightning Source LLC
Chambersburg PA
CBHW050425110726

47899CB00008B/2849